Farmyard Beat

by
Lindsey Craig

illustrations by
Marc Brown

Alfred A. Knopf

New York

For my amazing family
—L.C.

For our lovely dancing Isabella
—M.B.

THIS IS A BORZOI BOOK PUBLISHED BY ALFRED A. KNOPF

Text copyright © 2011 by Lindsey Craig
Jacket art and interior illustrations copyright © 2011 by Marc Brown

All rights reserved. Published in the United States
by Alfred A. Knopf, an imprint of Random House Children's Books,
a division of Random House, Inc., New York.

Knopf, Borzoi Books, and the colophon are registered
trademarks of Random House, Inc.

Visit us on the Web! www.randomhouse.com/kids

Educators and librarians, for a variety of teaching tools,
visit us at www.randomhouse.com/teachers

Library of Congress Cataloging-in-Publication Data
Craig, Lindsey.
Farmyard beat / by Lindsey Craig ; illustrations by Marc Brown.
p. cm.
Summary: The sounds of the farm animals create a lively beat that keeps
Farmer Sue, the chicks, sheep, and other farm animals awake.
ISBN 978-0-375-86455-1 (trade) — ISBN 978-0-375-96455-8 (lib. bdg.)
[1. Stories in rhyme. 2. Domestic animals—Fiction. 3. Bedtime—Fiction.]
I. Brown, Marc Tolon, ill. II. Title.
PZ8.3.C84367Far 2011   [E]—dc22   2010016123

The text of this book is set in 40-point and 60-point Arthur.
The illustrations in this book were created using hand-painted papers and a
collage technique that focused on cutting the paper into primary shapes.

MANUFACTURED IN CHINA
June 2011
10 9 8 7 6 5 4 3 2 1

First Edition

Peep-peep-peep!

Chicks can't sleep. Chicks can't sleep.
Chicks can't sleep
'cause they got that beat!

Peep! Peep! Peep-peep-peep!

Peep! Peep! Peep-peep-peep!

All that peeping wakes up . . . .

Sheep!
Sheep can't sleep.
Sheep can't sleep.
Sheep can't sleep
'cause they got that beat.

TAT! TAT! Tattity-tat-tat!

TAT! TAT! Tattity-tat-tat!

All that racket wakes up . . .

Cat!
Cat can't sleep.
Cat can't sleep.
Cat can't sleep
'cause she's got that beat.

Puuurrrr! Mee-ooow!

Puuurrrr! Mee-ooow!

All that racket wakes up . . .

Cow!
Cows can't sleep.
Cows can't sleep.
Cows can't sleep
'cause they got that beat.

SWISH! CLANK! Swish-swish! Clank!

SWISH! CLANK! Swish-swish! Clank!

All that racket wakes Ol' . . .

Hank!
Hank can't sleep.
Hank can't sleep.
Hank can't sleep
'cause he's got that beat.

Woof! How-WOOOOO!

Woof! How-WOOOOO!

All that racket wakes up . . .

Shhh! Shhh!
Look who's coming!

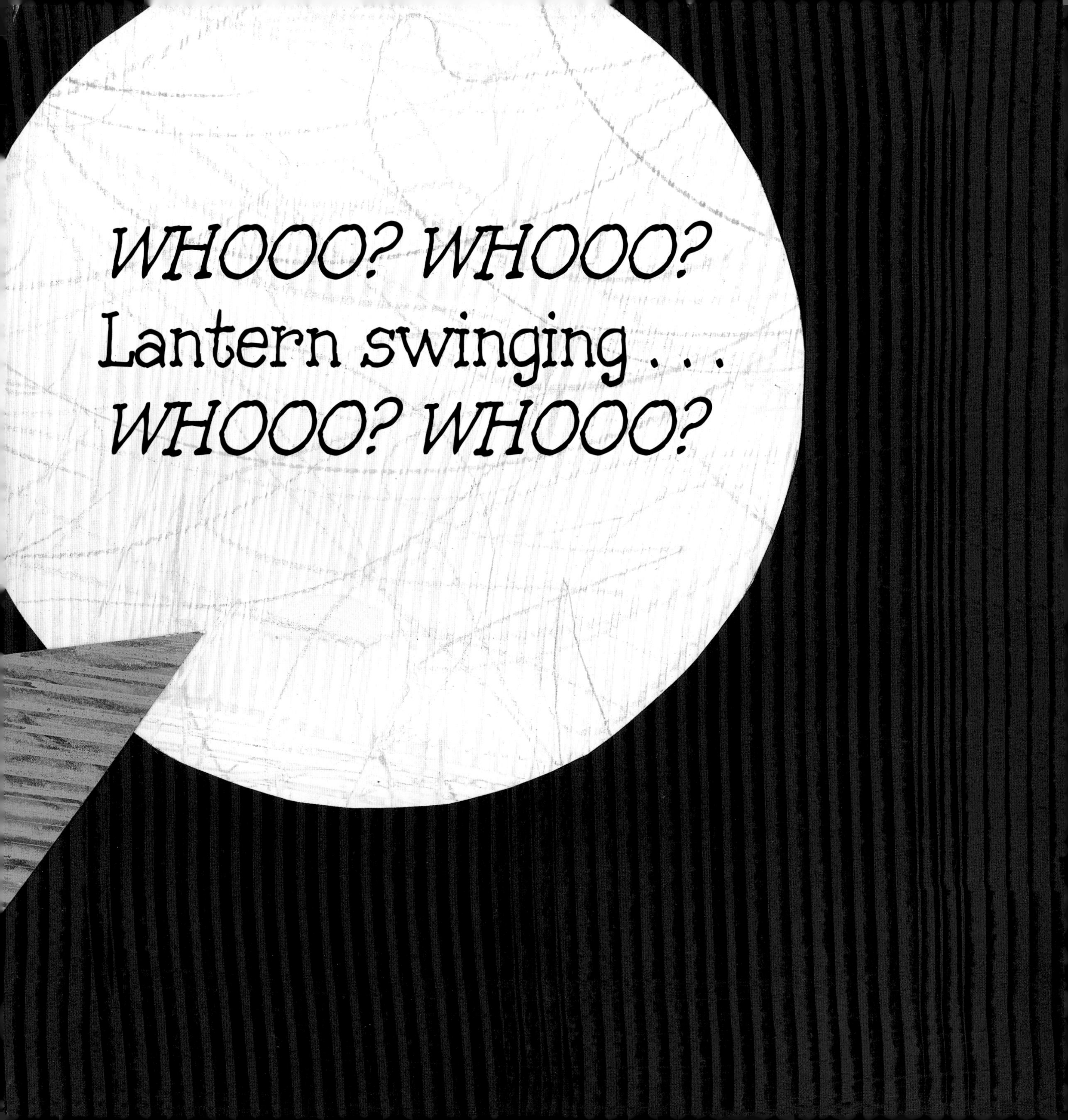

WHOOO? WHOOO?
Lantern swinging . . .
WHOOO? WHOOO?

FARMER SUE!!!

Sue can't sleep.

Sue can't sleep.

Sue can't sleep

'cause she's heard that beat.

Sue looks here! Sue looks there!

"No one here or anywhere!"

With a y-a-w-n, she thinks she'll go to sleep

when . . .

Peep! Peep!
Peep-peep-peep!
Chicks can't help it.
They got that beat!
Then . . .

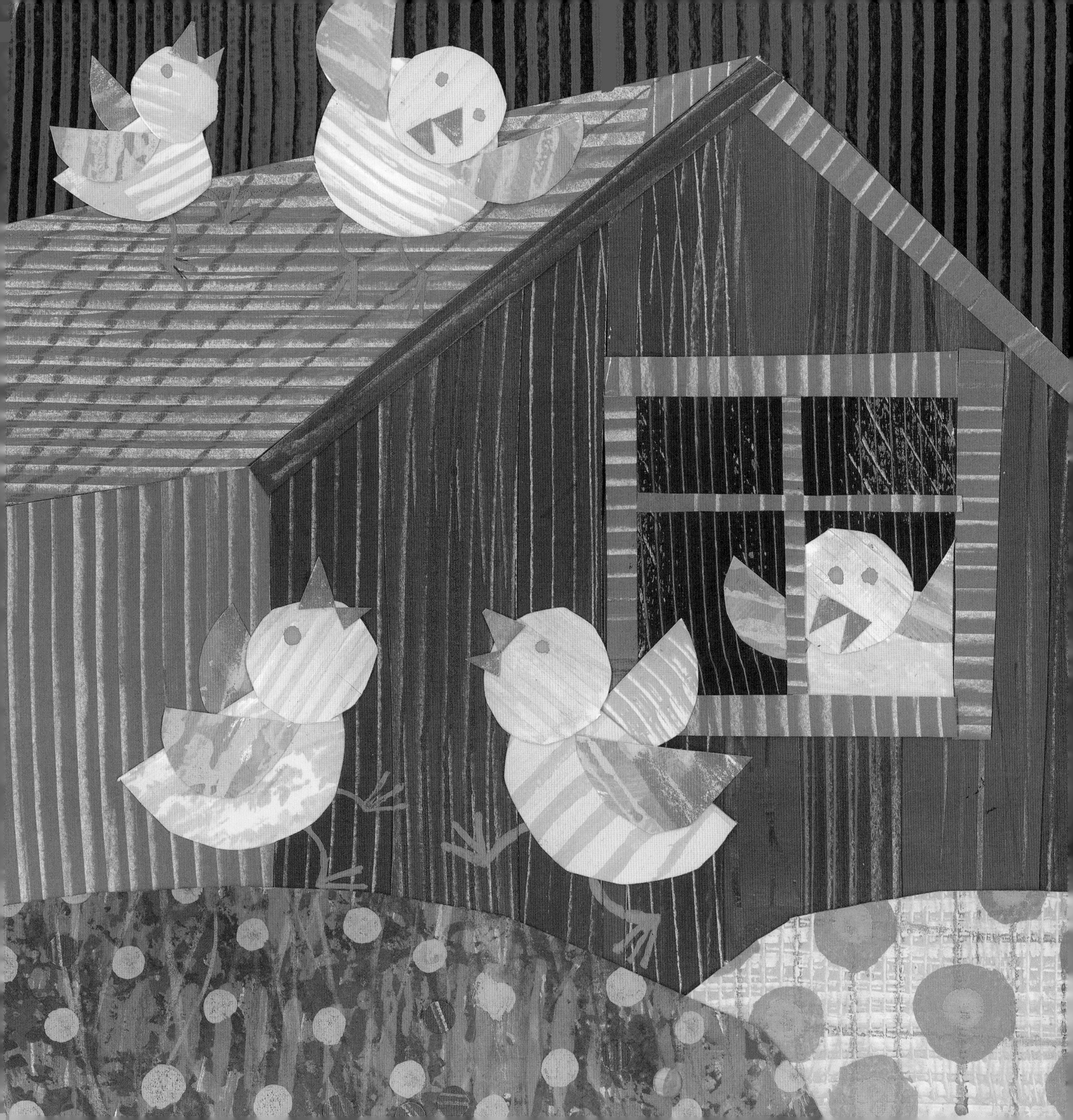

TAT! TAT! Tattity-tat-tat!

Puuurrrr! Mee-ooow!

SWISH! CLANK! Swish-swish! Clank!

Woof! How-WOOOOO!

WHOOO? WHOOO?

JIG! JIG! A-jiggity-jig!

Everyone's dancing to that beat.

T-I-L-L . . .

. . . they fall in a heap!

Asleep!